WAGONS HO!

1846

NOW

George Hallowell and **Joan Holub**   Illustrated by **Lynne Avril**

Albert Whitman & Company, Chicago, Illinois

For Margaret Questad, a true pioneer.—G.H. AND J.H.

To my dad, who through his stories gave me a love of history.—L.A.

Library of Congress Cataloging-in-Publication Data

Hallowell, George.
Wagons ho! / by George Hallowell and Joan Holub ; illustrated by Lynne Avril.
p. cm.
Summary: Compares the experiences of Jenny Johnson and Katie Miller as
their families move from Missouri to Oregon, one in 1846 and one in 2011.
ISBN 978-0-8075-8612-9
[1. Moving, Household—Fiction. 2. Overland journeys to the
Pacific—Fiction. 3. Wagon trains—Fiction. 4. Automobile travel—Fiction.]
I. Holub, Joan. II. Avril, Lynne, ill. III. Title.
PZ7.H159Wag 2011
[E]—dc22
2010050422

The design is by Carol Gildar.

For more information about Albert Whitman & Company,
please visit our web site at www.albertwhitman.com.

Would you have dared go west in 1846?

If you had, you'd be in for a long, dusty, tiring, flat, mountainous, wet, dry, boring, exciting, fun, terrifying trip. By land, you'd travel on the Oregon Trail, the longest trail in North America. In 1846, it would have taken you five days to travel as far as we can drive in one hour today!

So why would you go? Maybe you heard that a "great migration" to the West began in 1843 when nine hundred settlers traveled the Oregon Trail. Before that, the trail was only a rough path used by Native Americans and fur traders. At that time, Oregon didn't even belong to the United States! England wanted it, too. Maybe you heard that pioneers were getting six hundred forty free acres just for settling there. That much land was worth $800 in some parts of the United States. That was a lot of money in those days, when farm hands earned about $75 in a whole year. Or maybe you'd go because you heard the farmland was fertile or because you believed the wild stories about Oregon being an almost magical, perfect place.

You'd probably start your trip in Independence, Missouri, and end about two thousand miles west in the Oregon Country. You'd leave in April or May. By then, snow would have melted, and the trail wouldn't be too muddy. Grass would be growing so you could feed your livestock.

You'd go with other pioneers because that was safer. Most stories about trouble with Native Americans weren't true. But there were other dangers such as wild animals, bad weather, and accidents. You'd follow streams and rivers so you'd have water. Your wagon could go about fifteen miles each day. If it rained, mud would make it hard to go even one mile. You'd better hope you'd make it to the trail's end by September. Otherwise, you might get snowed in among the mountains and freeze or starve to death.

Still, like most pioneers, you'd probably think the new life you had found for yourself and your family was worth it in the end.

1846

Papa and Mama say we are moving! Right now, my family rents farmland in Independence, Missouri. We want free land near a town called Oregon City to build our own farm.

So we are going to head west to Oregon Country with hundreds of other pioneers. I've never been outside of Independence before!

Our trip will take five months, from May to September. I've heard that some people die on the trail. I hope we survive the journey.

Jenny

Livestock

My bed

Our farmhouse

Little brother feeding the chickens

Mama churning

My cat, Tabby

Me collecti... eggs

Papa plowing with our two oxen

NOW

Mom and Dad say we're moving! They've both gotten new jobs in Oregon City. That means we have to leave our home in Independence, Missouri.

I've lived here my whole life! I don't want to go. But nobody listens to me. We're moving to Oregon, and that's that.

We will leave on July 1st. Our trip will take five days, from Monday to Friday. I've never been on the road in a car for five whole days. All that driving—not to mention my brother driving me crazy the whole way. How will I survive?

Katie

Our house

My room

My thinking tree

Me calling my bff with the big news

My brother being a pest

My dog, Elly

Mom playing tennis

Dad on the computer, listening to music

1846

We are the Johnson family from Missouri. We are moving west.

This is me, Jenny.

Sunbonnet to keep from getting more freckles

Freckles

Calico dress made by Mama

My doll, Sue

Tabby

She's a good mouser.

Lulu, our milk cow

Flyswatter tail

Mr. Trouble, also known as Ned, my little brother

NOW

We are the Millers from Missouri. We are moving west.

This is me, Katie.

My doll, Lila. My bff gave her to me when I was five.

Cool pink glasses

Naturally curly hair

Glamorous T-shirt

Elly

Waggly tail

Her toy

Mr. Annoying, also known as Buddy, my little brother

If you want to make him steam, just call him Rosebud.

Papa buys two more oxen from a farmer. They will pull our wagon to Oregon.

I will call you Blossom.

1846

Flour

Sugar

Rice

Beans

Hardtack biscuits

Bacon

While Papa readies the wagon, we pack. Mama puts the dishes inside an oak barrel full of cornmeal so they won't break. Mama and I have to pack everything. Mr. Trouble is off playing hoop.

Bad Sad Tidings:

Papa says Tabby can't go to Oregon. I know he is right. She would get lost on the way, chasing mice. My cousin promises to take care of her. Still, I cry at losing her. Farewell, Mrs. Tabby Whiskers.

There is little room, and we must keep our load light. Many possessions get left behind:

Table

Armoire

Ned's rock collection

Mama's garden. (I will bring seeds with me.)

Papa's goat, pig, and three roosters are sold.

WAGONS HO!

Our guide calls . . .
It is time to depart.

Dad rents a trailer to carry what we will need when we first get to Oregon.

NOW

We hope everything will fit.

Dishes

Stuff

Linens

Books

Toys

The movers load all the furniture into their truck. Mom and I pack the suitcases. Mr. Annoying is no help at all.

Moving is killing me.

All I do is say goodbye. It's so hard to leave my thinking tree and my best pal, Sophie.

We can't take everything. It's time for a

Goodbye, previously enjoyed toys. (Just kidding—there's no way I'd sell Lila!)

YARD SALE!

Dad calls . . .

Ta-ta, chair.

LET'S GO!

Au revoir, old computer.

So long, clothes that don't fit.

And we're off . . .

MAY 1846

We take a raft across the river. It is exciting, but Ned is worried we might tip.

Have a safe journey!

KANSAS RIVER

MONDAY

Bob

WELCOME TO KANSAS

We drive over a bridge to Kansas.

KANSAS RIVER

The Henderson family lost everything in the crossing. We all share what we can to help them travel on.

The whole world is our bathroom. I go behind a bush.

Things we do every day of our journey:

1846

4 A.M.: Bugle wakes us.

5 A.M.: Round up cattle.

Milk Lulu.

5:30 A.M.: Light fire and cook breakfast.

7 A.M.: WAGONS HO!

NOONING. We eat breakfast leftovers.

I walk mostly. So do Mama and Mr. Trouble. Papa drives the wagon. It is so bumpy that it churns Lulu's milk to butter in one day!

Count buffalo.

Worry about getting LOST!

I miss Tabby.

Before dark, we find a good place to camp.

Mama and the ladies quilt and mend. They also make supper. We do chores. Then there is music and talking.

Count stars.

Things we do every day of our trip:

NOW

7 A.M.

Rise and shine! That's what Dad tells us.

Breakfast at a café.

Put gas in Bob.

GAS

MAP USA

Get out the maps.

Write in our travel journals. I miss my bff.

Drive. Drive. Drive.

More driving.

ALASKA CWG 500

HAWAII KTE 268 ALOHA STATE

We play the license plate game. Alaska and Hawaii are hard to find.

This is what we look like in the back seat.

Me

Mr. Annoying

Do not cross!

Walk Elly.

We stay in a hotel with a pool!

Count stars.

JUNE 1846

Maps are not always accurate.
Huzzah! We see Chimney Rock.
That means we are on the right trail.

Mama
Ned
Me
Papa

TUESDAY

Are we going the right way?
Yep. We cruise through
Nebraska and into
Wyoming.

North Platte
next right

SPEED
LIMIT
50

CHIMNEY ROCK
(because it's tall like a chimney)

FORT LARAMIE

Many tribes trade here.

We stock up on supplies at the trading post.

CORN MEAL xxx

CORN

100 LB BEANS

Papa mails a letter I wrote to ask how Tabby is.

Dear Carrie
How is Mrs. Tabby Cat? I miss her.
Love,
Jenny

We have come one third of the distance. But we don't tarry. We must reach Independence Rock by July 4th if we're to cross the mountains before the winter snow.

Big Joe's Trading Post

We don't trade anything.
We buy stuff.

Postcard

CHIMNEY ROCK

Snack

CHIPS

PIONEER GIRL

Moccasins

LUNCH SNACKS SOUVENIRS

Hey! The girl in this book is taking the same trip we are!

PIONEER GIRL

The weather guy on TV says a storm is coming. Dad makes us get up early Wednesday morning. He wants to get going before it hits.

Me, very sleepy

JULY 1846

We have arrived at Independence Rock in good time. Now we will beat the snow to Oregon. Slow snow. Ha! Ha!

INDEPENDENCE ROCK
(because pioneers try to get here by Independence Day)

I bet my name carving will be here for a hundred years

LEE

J.H. BAUGHMAN

NED 1846

R.L. WINSHIP 1825

WEDNESDAY

The storm didn't catch us! We stop at Independence Rock, in Wyoming, on July 4th. It's not as big as I expected.

Let's climb to the top and see where the pioneers wrote their names.

JULY & AUGUST 1846

Some wagons are too heavy to go up and down the mountains. Many things must be given up in order to cross. The Rockies look like a graveyard of precious belongings left by many families going west.

1846

This trip is so long. Every week seems like a year! We have so many troubles on the way.

The oxen's feet are sore. We make moccasins for them.

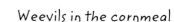

We can't find wood, so we use buffalo chips to fuel our cooking fires.

I tire of eating beans and hardtack.

Weevils in the cornmeal

I miss my friends. I miss Tabby Whiskers. I hope things are easier once we reach Oregon.

My boots are wearing thin.

Stuck in the mud—again.

AUGUST 1846

The Rockies are behind us.
We are all so happy.
One night around the campfire,
I make a new friend.
Her name is Lucy.

Lucy teaches me to play "Skip to My Lou."

THURSDAY

We made it through the Idaho Rockies in time for a swim at our hotel. And guess what? I made a new friend named Luciana.

We like the same shows.

We pick berries and make berry pie.

Lucy's family is leaving the wagon train and going to California.

Goodbye.   Goodbye.

Moving means saying lots of goodbyes. I hope it's worth it in the end.

We scream for ice cream.
Both of us get mint chocolate chip.

Luciana's family lives in California. So tomorrow they'll go one way, we another.

Bye. I'll text you.

Awesome. Bye!

SEPTEMBER 1846

At last! We arrive
at Oregon City.
We are tired, but happy
to have survived
our journey.
Still, we have no home yet.
What now?

By October,
we stake a land
claim near the
Willamette River.

Papa clears the land
and hauls the logs
to our building site.

A CAT!

He wanders in from
the forest. Papa says
I can keep him.

One chewed ear

Calico colors

I will name him Patches.

FRIDAY

Yay! We made it to Oregon City. Buddy and I high five. We are so glad to get out of the car for good. What's next?

This house is just right for us. There's even a tree like my old thinking tree back home.

MY DOLL!

The hotel found Lila and sent her to us.

My bff texted me! I send her a picture of my new room.

1846

It's cabin-raising day!
Neighbors come from miles around. The men
bring their tools. Women bring baskets of food.
With all the help, our cabin is built in one day!

It is almost rainy season, so we
are glad when the roof is on!
We have a party with fiddles,
food, and fun. I dance the
Virginia Reel with Mr. Trouble.

This is Elsa from New York.
She knows a good swimming hole.
We eat watermelon and practice
spitting seeds.

NOW

We have take-out chicken in our empty house. Buddy says I have chicken legs. How annoying!

The truck comes with our stuff! Zack, Jack, and Joe unload everything. I help show them where it goes.

This is Lissa from down the street. She does not have an annoying brother—she has an annoying sister!

1846

Our wheat farm will be planted here next spring. I will grow sunflowers with seeds from our old garden.

New friend is two miles that way.

The schoolhouse is too far away. I will learn at home.

Oregon City has a sawmill, blacksmith shop, a tinsmith, and a gristmill.

My bed

Lulu

Ned's new rock collection has only one rock so far, from the Rocky Mountains.

I embroider a gift for Mama and Papa . . .

HOME SWEET HOME

NOW

New school is that way.

The mall is that way.

New friend is two blocks that way.

Buddy has found a nutty buddy.

My room

I miss Sophie and my old tree, but this is starting to feel like . . .

Home Sweet Home!